This Little Tiger book belongs to:

_____

_____

_____

_____

For Talia, with love from Granny D.
And with thanks to Deborah Kilcollins,
who sparked this story
~ D H

For Marianne, my wonderful oodle doodle
apple strudel mum
~ S M

LITTLE TIGER PRESS
An imprint of Magi Publications
1 The Coda Centre, 189 Munster Road,
London SW6 6AW
www.littletigerpress.com

First published in Great Britain 2008
This edition published 2008

Text copyright © Diana Hendry 2008
Illustrations copyright © Sarah Massini 2008
Diana Hendry and Sarah Massini have asserted their rights
to be identified as the author and illustrator of this work
under the Copyright, Designs and Patents Act, 1988

A CIP catalogue record for this book
is available from the British Library

ISBN 978-1-84506-450-1

Printed in Singapore

10 9 8 7 6 5 4 3 2 1

Oodles of Noodles Oodles of Noodles Oodles of Noodles Oodles of Noodles Oodles of Noodles Oodles of Noodles Oodles of Noodles Oodles of Noodles Oodles of Noodles Oodles of Noodles Oodles of Noodles Oodles of Noodles Oodles of Noodles Oodles of Noodles Oodles of Noodles Oodles of Noodles

Diana Hendry
illustrated by Sarah Massini

Oodles of Noodles Oodles of Noodles Oodles of Noodles Oodles of Noodles Oodles of Noodles Oodles of Noodles Oodles of N

Oodles of Noodles Oodles of Noodles Oodles of Noodles Oodles of Noodles Oodles of Noodles Oodles of Noodles Oodles of Noodles Oodles

LITTLE TIGER PRESS
London

On her birthday Mrs Mungo was given a **pasta-making machine**. "*Noodles* for dinner, *noodles* for tea, *noodles* for you and *noodles* for me!" sang Mrs Mungo.

"I like **Chips**," said Lily.

"And **burgers**," said Ben.

$\mathbf{M}$rs Mungo put the **pasta-making machine** on the kitchen table, fetched a bowl and made a **HUGE** ball of pasta dough.

"*Noodles* with garlic, *noodles* with *jam*!" she sang.

"Chips with salt and vinegar," said Lily. "And burgers," said Ben.

When Lily and Ben had gone to school, Mrs Mungo began **rolling** out the pasta. It was **HARD** work turning the handle of the machine and **rolling** the pasta thinner and thinner.

"**Never mind**," said Mrs Mungo. "I'll soon have

oodles of *noodles*."

And at that something *very* **STRANGE** happened. The **pasta machine** began working all by itself.

Long, long loops of *noodles* rolled out of the **machine**. Very soon Mrs Mungo was tucked up **tight** in a *noodle* sleeping bag.

At school there was
noodles, **onions**
and **peas** for lunch.

Lily and Ben ate
the **onions** and **peas**.

At home the **pasta machine** worked *faster* and *faster*. Soon *noodles* twirled **round** the bannisters . . .

dangled from the shower rail . . .

and *tied* the television up in knots.

Mrs Mungo **struggled** to free her arms.

"**STOP! STOP!**" Mrs Mungo cried to the **pasta machine**. But it didn't.

"There must be a magic word," thought Mrs Mungo.

"*Doodle!*" she shouted. "*Poodle* and *doodle* and *apple strudel!*" she **shouted**.

But the **pasta machine** took **no** notice.

Instead the *noodles* *slithered* under the door and OUT down the path.

Outside the house, *noodles* wound themselves **round** the garden gates, **wriggled round** lamp posts and *dangled* from trees.

Very soon *everyone* in the street
came out and began filling their
saucepans with *noodles*.

The *noodles* ran on down the road until they reached the school. The children were in the playground. They thought the *noodles* were *wonderful*. They made *noodle* skipping ropes and *noodle* hoops – all except Lily and Ben.

"*Noodles!*" cried Ben.

"*Oodles* and *oodles* and *oodles* of *noodles!*" cried Lily.

"Quick, Ben! Home! I think Mum needs us."

And as fast as they could, Lily and Ben ran.
It wasn't easy.

When at last they reached the kitchen, the *pasta machine* was still ***WHIZZING*** out *noodles*.

They kept tripping over the noodles and bumping into noodle collectors.

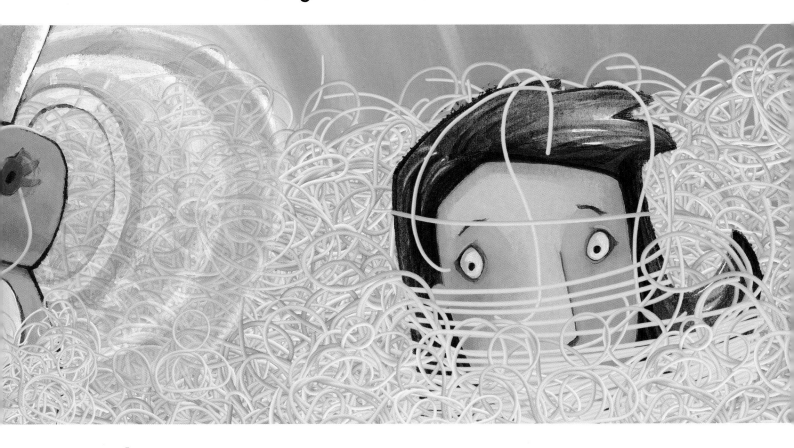

All they could see of their mother was her head. She was totally noodled.

"**It won't stop!**" wept Mrs Mungo. "All I said was '*Oodles* of *noodles*' and it *noodled* and **noodled** and **noodled**. I've tried every magic word I know."

"I don't suppose you tried saying it the other way round, did you?" asked Ben.

"**I didn't think of that**," said his mother.

So all together and very loudly, they said, "*Noodles* of *oodles!*" And with a groan of relief, the **pasta machine** stopped.

Ben and Lily unwrapped their
mother. She *flopped* in a chair
as Lily wound the
noodles into a
great big ball.

"I suppose it's *noodles* for tea," said Lily. "**Oh no!**" said Mrs Mungo. "It isn't. It's chips. Chips and burgers."

Have *oodles* of fun

with stories from Little Tiger Press

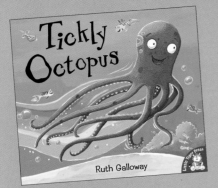

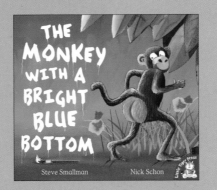

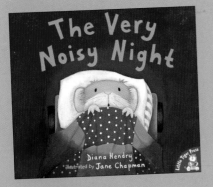

For information regarding any of the above
titles or for our catalogue, please contact us:
Little Tiger Press, 1 The Coda Centre,
189 Munster Road, London SW6 6AW, UK
Tel: 020 7385 6333 • Fax: 020 7385 7333
E-mail: info@littletiger.co.uk • www.littletigerpress.com